FAT LEOPARD

BY

CHERYL RICHARDSON

ILLUSTRATED BY

TREY BROADBENT

ISBN: 978-1-60594-565-1 (PB)

Printed in the United States of America by Llumina Press

Library of Congress Control Number: 2010909314

Dedicated to my sisters Sandy and Brenda, my heroines (girl heroes)

"Sticks and stones will break your bones, but names can never hurt you." My mama always told me that, but it was not true. Words do hurt, and they hurt deep down, deep down in your soul.

I was not an only child, but I grew up as one. My sisters were ten and twelve years older. Mama always said I was a surprise. Surprises are good things. For a lot of my life, it was just me, my mama, and my daddy.

My sisters were my heroines. You know, those are girl heroes. They were majorettes. I always wanted to be a majorette.

I watched them twirl their batons. They would weave their batons around their necks. They would weave their batons between their legs. They would throw their batons so high in the air that they could turn around three times and still catch them. Sometimes they would twirl special batons that they would dip in kerosene. When it got dark, they would weave their magic in the nighttime sky. I would tell everyone that they were my sisters. I wanted to be a majorette, just like them.

I practiced and practiced, but it just wasn't easy for me. I could throw the baton high in the air, but by the time I turned around, I did not catch it. Sometimes it would even hit me on the head. I was slow, because I was chubby.

My sisters were queens of everything. They wore fluffy dresses in many colors. They looked so pretty in those dresses. I wanted a fluffy dress. I wanted to be a queen, but I was chubby.

My mom bought me fluffy dresses for Easter. She even bought me bonnets every year. I liked my fluffy dresses. I liked my bonnets too, but I did not look like my sisters, because I was chubby.

My sisters rode on floats in parades. They waved the "queen wave" even when they were not queens. I practiced that wave when I watched them in parades. I wanted to ride on a float. I wanted to wave the "queen wave."

When I was eight, I rode on a float in the parade. I waved the "queen wave," but I was not a queen. Many people smiled and waved back, but I heard them say, "Look, she is so cute and chubby!"

My sisters had boyfriends. I wanted a boyfriend. They danced with their boyfriends. I danced too. I had pretend boyfriends. One time I even kissed my pretend boyfriend, just like I saw my sister do! I picked my pretend boyfriends out of their high school yearbook. Someday, I would have a real boyfriend when I was not chubby.

I always liked boys. When I was in the first grade, I fell in love. He was not chubby. He was very skinny. He was short. I was tall and chubby. He had pretty brown eyes. They were sad eyes. I wondered why his eyes were so sad. I looked at him all day long. He never looked back.

One day our teacher told us we were going to have a Valentine's Day contest. We were to decorate boxes which would hold our valentines. My daddy helped me make my box. It was wrapped in white tissue paper. It had bright red hearts all over it and one special big red heart that opened up like an accordion. There was a slit on top that made it like a mailbox. Everyone would put my valentines in that mailbox. It won first place. It made my daddy proud, me too!

Valentine's Day had one rule. If you were going to participate, you had to make a valentine for everybody in the room, even those that were chubby. I liked that rule. "Sad Eyes" participated, so I was going to get a valentine from him.

Valentine's Day arrived. Everyone in the class participated. That made me happy. I looked through all of my cards until I found it. I had hoped it would say, "Love, Sad Eyes," but it just had his name. That was okay, because it was a pretty card, and now I had a boyfriend!

My mom and dad went to Florida. They left me in the care of my sisters. My sisters took good care of me. They dressed me up like you do your baby dolls. One day they sent me to school in a frosted wig. I do not know how Mrs. McBride knew my parents were on vacation.

My sister went away to college that next year. She went far away to Tennessee. I was so sad. She was my best friend. Why did she have to go so far away? Maybe she didn't like me anymore.

One day I got a telephone call from Tennessee. My sister had been selected Homecoming Queen. She wanted me to walk her out onto the football field. She was proud of me even though I was chubby.

My mom and I went shopping. It took a long time, but when I saw it, I knew it was the "Just Right" outfit. I rounded the corner and saw the prettiest coat in the whole wide world. It had a matching hat. It was made of leopard printed fur. They even had it in my size which was 6X. The X stood for chubby. My mom liked it too. I could not wait until I could wear it to school. It was a happy day!

When I got home my mom told me that I could not wear it to school. She told me I had to wait and wear it to Tennessee. Now my happy turned very, very sad.

The day finally arrived. We headed out in our big, black Ford to Tennessee. The roads were so winding. I almost threw up. It was not a happy trip like I had thought. It was a long curvy trip. I thought we would never get there.

When I got there, I could not see my sister. She said there was no room in her dorm for me. We would have to stay in the Blue Circle Motel. This was not a happy time!

The alarm clock chirped like a bird. I bounded out of bed. The air was very chilly, just perfect for my leopard coat. When I got to Maryville College, she was waiting for me in the parking lot. This was a happy day, because she liked my coat, and she still liked me. She took me to meet her friends. They liked my coat, and they liked me. She was getting her crown at two o'clock. That was five long hours away.

At one o'clock we had practice. I was good at practice. At two o'clock I proudly walked her onto the field. The crowd smiled. They liked my coat. They liked me, even though I was chubby. They put a crown on her head. She was a queen. I was very proud, even though I was not a queen.

It was a good trip home. The roads did not seem so curvy. It did not seem to take as long to get home. I did not get sick. When I got home my mama told me the very best news of all. She told me that I could wear my coat and hat to school. I was so excited that I dreamed about it. I dreamed that everybody smiled and liked my coat. They all wanted to touch it because it was so soft.

At the bus stop the next morning, no one smiled or wanted to touch my coat. They just giggled. No one smiled or asked to touch my coat when I got to school. No one said anything about my coat, except Mrs. McBride. She said I looked lovely. I felt lovely, until...

RECESS. At recess we played tag. "Sad Eyes" was it. I ran slowly so he could catch me. When he caught me, I was so happy until...

Those horrible, horrible words came out of his mouth. When he tagged me he shouted, "I got Fat Leopard!" Those words stung in my ears. They stung in my heart. They stung deep down in my soul. Sticks and stones can break your bones, but those two words did hurt me. The other kids liked those words. They caught fire, like my sister's kerosene dipped batons. Everyone was shouting them. I wanted to run away. I wanted to hide. I tried to pretend that they were saying those words because they liked me. I kept playing so I would not cry. I did not want anyone to know how badly I hurt.

When I got home, I threw my coat and hat in the closet. I told my mama that I did not want to wear it to school anymore. My mama did not understand. The coat only came out of the closet for church, because at church no one called me "Fat Leopard." The coat looked very lonely in the closet. This was not a happy time.

One Saturday morning the worst thing happened. There was a knock at my door. I ran to see who was there. It was HIM! "Sad Eyes" peeked through the door as I peeked back. When I opened the door, the most horrible thing happened. He shouted, "Run, or Fat Leopard will sit on you!" Those were very, very bad words. He ran down the street laughing with his friend. This was a very, very bad day!

This day was so bad that I felt it deep, deep down in my soul. My mama's face looked like she felt it too. Now she understood why the coat had to hang in the closet.

I did not want to wear the coat, and I did not want to go to school. I hated the coat, I hated school, and I hated me.

The sadder I got, the chubbier I got. My sisters put me on a diet. This was not a happy time. I liked donuts, and I liked cupcakes. Diets do not have donuts and cupcakes. The diets did not work. By the time I was in the third grade, I was not chubby; I was fat.

During the summer of my fifth grade year, something happened. I still ate cupcakes. I still ate donuts, but every morning I woke up a little thinner. It was like someone was stretching me. It was kind of like one those butterflies that we had studied in school. It starts out like a chubby worm, and then one day it wakes up a beautiful butterfly. I thought maybe it was a trick, but when I went back to school after summer, everyone thought I was a new girl in school. "Sad Eyes" had moved away. I was sad, because I wanted to see if he thought I looked like a butterfly.

In junior high, I ran for student council. My daddy helped me with my campaign. “DON'T BE CONTRARY, VOTE FOR SHERRY!” Boy, did I have a clever daddy. His campaign slogan and campaign cards with candy attached did the trick. I won the election. My daddy helped me win the Valentine's Day contest, he sold my Girl Scout cookies, and now he had helped me win the election. I had a good daddy!

Junior high was filled with happy times. I did not want for boyfriends. Everyone likes a butterfly.

High school was mostly filled with happy times." Sad Eyes" returned to my school. I still wanted to be a queen so badly. I was nominated for the homecoming court. My mama was excited because my sisters had been queens. She thought it would be nice if I could be a queen, too. I did not want to be a disappointment to my mama.

When they picked the court, they would call all the nominees into a room and then announce the winners. What if I did not get it? What if I cried? I would hate for anyone to know how badly I wanted to win. My mama told me to just remember how blessed I was. She told me to think about boys and girls who were missing arms and legs. Well, as they started to call names, I got a lump in my throat. The more I thought about those armless boys and girls, the bigger the lump got. At last the lump exploded, and tears streamed down my face. I did not get to be on the homecoming court. How could wanting to be a queen be so important?

Being skinny did not last long. The strangest thing was that when I looked into the mirror I was not skinny, but I still saw a butterfly. I guess all that love my mama, daddy, and sisters had for me, made me show love to everyone else. That love was what made me a butterfly. Anyone can be a butterfly.

In my senior year, "Sad Eyes" was voted king of the prom. Guess what? I was voted queen. No longer was I Fat Leopard. I was finally a queen. I got to do the "queen wave" with my king.

LaVergne, TN USA
26 December 2010
210055LV00004B

* 9 7 8 1 6 0 5 9 4 5 6 5 1 *